*For Heath.*
*Thank you for laughing at my bedtime stories*
*and helping me to make up Pinky Dinky Doo.*

Special thanks to Katonah Elementary School

Photography by Sandra Kress

Digital coloring and compositing by Alisa Klayman-Grodsky

Photo credit: monkey image on p. 12 and p. 41 © Bettmann/CORBIS.

www.stepintoreading.com

Educators and librarians, for a variety of teaching tools, visit us at
www.randomhouse.com/teachers

*Library of Congress Cataloging-in-Publication Data*
Jinkins, Jim.
Pinky Dinky Doo : Polka Dot Pox / by Jim Jinkins.
   p.   cm. — (Step into reading. A step 3 book)
SUMMARY: When her brother catches a cold, Pinky Dinky Doo, an imaginative young girl, tells him a silly story about the time she and her classmates caught the Polka Dot Pox.
ISBN 0-375-82915-6 (trade) — ISBN 0-375-92713-1 (lib. bdg.) — ISBN 0-375-82713-7 (pbk.)
[1. Sick—Fiction.   2. Brothers and sisters—Fiction.   3. Show-and-tell presentations—Fiction.
4. Imagination—Fiction.   5. Storytelling—Fiction.]
I. Title.   II. Series: Step into reading. Step 3 book.
PZ7.J57526Pg   2004   [E]—dc21   2003004027

Printed in the United States of America   10 9 8 7 6 5 4 3 2 1

Polka Dot Pox

by Jim Jinkins

Random House New York

Mommy Doo

Daddy Doo

Mr. Guinea Pig

Tyler Doo

Pinky Dinky Doo

Daffinee Toilette

Nicholas Biscuit

Bobby Boom

"Time for bed," Pinky Dinky Doo
said to her brother, Tyler.

"Tell me a story, Pinky," he begged.

"Sure! Let me think one up,"
said Pinky.

Just then, Tyler let out a huge

"It sounds like you're getting a cold,"
Pinky said.

"Duh-huh," Tyler said

through his stopped-up nose.

"Let me tell you a story about

a girl named Pinky Dinky Doo,"

said Pinky.

"That will make you feel better.

I'll just shut my eyes,

wiggle my ears,

and crank up my imagination!"

The name of this story is . . .

# Polka Dot Pox

A made-up story
by Pinky Dinky Doo

Oh, goody.
Here we go!

It was evening in

# Great Big City.

Pinky Dinky Doo was all done
with the yummy dinner
Daddy Doo had made.

Now it was homework time!

Pinky was so excited about
school the next day.
It was finally her turn
for pet show-and-tell!

Yesterday Nicholas Biscuit brought
in his monkey, Professor Funky.
He slapped his head to the tune of
"Yankee Doodle Dandy"!

Slap! Slap!

And called it macaroni!

Bobby Boom showed
off his pet guppy,
Hush Puppy.
Hush Puppy could
do a triple flip!

The day before,
Daffinee Toilette brought
in her butler, Jinkins.
He was leading Daffinee's
pretty pink pet pony, Peaches.
Peaches did a perky prance
in a pair of purple underpants.

Pinky didn't have a guppy

or a monkey or a pretty pink pony.

All she had was her guinea pig,

Mr. Guinea Pig.

Pinky thought he was pretty cool.

He liked to eat carrots and

sleep all day and zoom around

on his exercise wheel.

But was he cool enough?

How could Pinky make him

a really, *really* cool pet?

"I know!" Pinky shouted.

"I can hook up his exercise wheel

to a popcorn popper.

The wheel can power the popper.

Squeek-
Squeeka

Squeek-
Squeeka

My pet guinea pig will make

snacks for the whole class!"

Kids, don't try this except in a made-up story.

Pinky Dinky Doo worked on the popper for the whole rest of the evening. Mr. Guinea Pig helped.

I said, bring me DUCT TAPE, not duck cake!

That night
Pinky gave
Mr. Guinea Pig
a bubble bath.

She painted
his teeny-tiny
toenails.

She brushed his fur
one hundred and
twenty-two times.

Mmm . . . fluffy!

Then Pinky and Mr. Guinea Pig
fell asleep right away
so the next day
would come sooner.

The next day was a perfect day
for show-and-tell.
As usual, Mr. Guinea Pig went
to give Pinky Dinky Doo
a great big good-morning kiss.
But when he saw her face,
he jumped clean out of his fur!
He ran back into his cage
and dove under the
cedar chips.

"That's strange," said Pinky.

"Hey, Tyler, did you see that?"

Tyler leaned over the bed rail.

When he saw Pinky's face,

he yelled, "Hokey jokey!" and

jumped clean out of his pajamas.

"I wonder why he did that," Pinky said.

She walked to the bathroom

and looked in the mirror.

She saw great big polka dots

all over her face!

"OH NO!" she shouted.

"I've got the Polka Dot Pox!

What about school?

What about show-and-tell?"

Pinky ran to show Mommy Doo.

When Mommy Doo saw Pinky,

she told Pinky to . . .

A Spin like a tornado
until the dots
flew off.

B

Cover her dots
with mashed
potatoes.

C Stay home from
school until she
was well again.

Pinky tried A and B.
But she got dizzy from spinning
and she didn't have any gravy.
So Pinky had to go with C.

Missing school was bad.
But missing her day to show off
Mr. Guinea Pig was bad news
times four!

Maybe Pinky could *sneak* out
of the house.

"I'll disguise myself," said Pinky.

She looked around the room.

"Let's see. Shoes, dirty socks,

underpants . . ."

Then Pinky

spotted her

costume box

in the corner.

Choose three things that make up
a good disguise for Pinky.

Eye Patch

Pirate Hat

Leafy Branch

Fake Nose & Glasses

Swashbuckling Boots

Football Shirt

Beatles Wig

Moose Antlers

That's right!

Pinky dressed up like a pirate.

Mr. Guinea Pig
was her parrot.

"Mommy Doo and Daddy Doo
will never know it's me," Pinky said.

Pinky was happy.

Life was perfect.

"Swag" means stuff that pirates steal, like gold and jewels.

And popcorn?

Life was not perfect.

Mommy Doo and Daddy Doo knew

they were raising a little girl—

not a pirate who sails

the high seas in search of swag!

So instead of pretending to be a pirate,

Pinky was a sick person in bed . . .

FOR REAL!

Pinky felt as stuck as a flower

in a flowerpot.

That gave her a great idea!

"My teacher, Ms. Maganza,

loves flowers," Pinky said.

"I'll turn myself into

a beautiful flower.

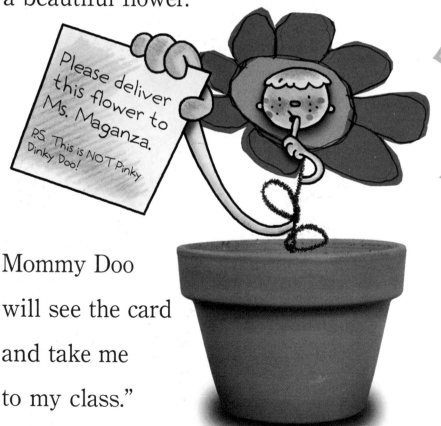

Please deliver this flower to Ms. Maganza.
P.S. This is NOT Pinky Dinky Doo!

Mommy Doo

will see the card

and take me

to my class."

Once again everything was perfect.
Mommy Doo carried the flowerpot
down the stairs.
But then Tyler started sneezing.
Pretend flowers made him
sneeze . . .
a lot!

He blew the petals
right off Pinky's head.
Pinky knew she was going nowhere.

Pinky had to let her teacher
know she was sick.
She called the school.
A machine answered
the phone with the most
surprising news.

This is the Great Big School. If you are in Ms. Maganza's class, please do NOT come to school today. Everybody has the Polka Dot Pox.

"My whole class has
the same thing I do!" Pinky said.
She thought about her friends.
"I wish there was something
I could do to help them
feel better."
If only they could see
Mr. Guinea Pig.
That would make
them feel better
for sure.
"I'm gonna have to

Pinky began to think.

She thought and thought

and thought and thought!

Normally, Pinky had an everyday,

kid-sized brain . . .

until she used it to

think big!

As her brain

filled up with ideas,

it got bigger and bigger . . .

Pinky, be sure to straighten up when you're finished thinking.

Okay, Mom!

until it filled the room.

And then it happened.

Pinky had a great big idea!

She bounced around the house
like a ball in a pinball machine.
Finally,
she landed
on the floor.

Which path leads to Pinky?

LIVING R

36

BEDROOM AREA

AREA

DN

ENTRY AREA

POW

Pinky told Mr. Guinea Pig
her really big idea.
"I'm going to . . .

**A** Flush myself
down the potty.

**B** Honk like a goose
and fly south for the winter.

**C** Invite my whole polka-dotted class
and their pets to my house
for a Polka Dot Party!"

To: Ms. Maganza's Class
From: Pinky Dinky Doo
   You are all invited to my house for a Polka Dot Party. Bring your pet. Popcorn will be served.

-Pinky Dinky Doo

The answer was C , of course.

If it was okay with Mommy

and Daddy Doo.

The next thing Pinky knew,
Bobby Boom,
Nicholas Biscuit,

40

and all the rest of the
class were crammed into
Pinky's room.

They laughed and had fun
playing connect-the-polka-dots
with each other.

Everybody thought Mr. Guinea Pig
was very cute.

Pinky got ready for show-and-tell.

She hooked Mr. Guinea Pig's wheel

to the popcorn popper.

He was ready to run!

Mr. Guinea Pig ran and ran and ran.

Squeek-Squeeka,
Squeek-Squeeka

And then, all of a sudden,

Pop!... Pop-Pop!... Pop-Pop-Pop!

It worked!

Mr. Guinea Pig made enough

popcorn for everybody.

All of Pinky Dinky Doo's friends

thought Mr. Guinea Pig was the

coolest pet ever!

"And that's exactly what
happened . . . sort of,"
Pinky said.
"That was a great story!"
said Tyler.
"I feel a lot better."

Pinky said, "I knew that story
would make you feel . . .
ahh . . . you feel . . .
ahhh . . . feel . . . ACHOO!"
Mr. Guinea Pig looked at Pinky.
She sneezed twice more.

"Uh-oh," Tyler said.

"I guess it's my turn.

I'll make up a story

to help you feel better, too!"

And that's exactly

what he did.